7 dark tales

7 dark tales

Christine Grace

Illustrated by Wendy Straw

A BROLLY BOOK

Dedication

This book is dedicated to my loving parents
Neville and Patricia Grace.

— Christine Grace

Brolly Books
(an imprint of Borghesi and Adam Publishers Pty Ltd)
Suite 330, 45 Glenferrie Road, Malvern Australia 3145
www.brollybooks.com
email: emma@brollybooks.com

First published in 2018. Reprinted 2019.

Text by Christine Grace.
Illustrations by Wendy Straw.
Cover design by Wendy Straw.
Internal page design and book specifications by Emma Borghesi.

Printed in China
ISBN 9781925386844
9781925386721 (pbk)

Publisher's Note

7 Dark Tales is written in prose poetry form,
with a focus on imagery and rhythm.
Therefore, conventional grammar rules have not been applied
where to do so would disturb the poetic effect.

A catalogue record for this
book is available from the
National Library of Australia

Contents

Cinder's Sister

She cut off her toe. With a carving knife from the dresser.

After the Prince had left. After the servant girl vanished. After her mother and sister had drunk the wine from the cellar. It was only then, when the house lay quiet, that she went down to the kitchen, took the knife from the top drawer dresser, and cut off her toe.

By the time the doctor arrived she was seeing worms dangling from the kitchen ceiling. The doctor stitched her up and gave her a stern talking-to.

Then he packed his kit and slammed the door.

Her mother and sister could not believe what she had done. They spat at her, then threw the pots from the kitchen mantle at her, cursing, 'You stupid, stupid girl! Don't you know the servant girl is getting married?'

She limped up the stairs and into her bedroom.

The door shut tight behind her. She clawed at the mattress until she had made a hole. She stuck her head right in it. She wanted to suffocate amongst the goose and duck but the feathers in the bed were no good for it. Eventually, she fell asleep.

When she woke it was snowing feathers. Her head felt thick and warm. She imagined she was a feather princess. With a feathery prince and castle.

She stayed there, with her head in the bed until she could bear it no longer. She kept thinking of the slipper and the way her foot had slipped right into it.

Except for that toe. That rotten little toe.

She crawled to the mirror. She looked crazed, like a half plucked chicken. Feathers sticking out at strange angles. Her face pale and puffy.

And her toe hurt too. Her ghost toe.
Her phantom toe.

Back down in the kitchen she went.
Over by the grate, in the ash, her little toe lay.
Shrivelled, bluish pink, like a slug.

'Oh, oh,' she cried, and she held it in her fingers and rocked it like a baby.

'There you are!' her mother breezed in. 'What are you doing, sitting in the grate, like the servant girl?
Get up, change your dress, do your hair. We are off to the Palace to meet the King and Queen.'

'And stop limping,' snarled her sister.

Bundled up in the carriage she was, her hair
brusquely set by the second servant girl who had
snivelled and snorted and told her that she'd seen
the magic woman who had made a mouse a man.

'What magic woman? What mouse man?'

But the servant girl had shrugged and her mother
had shouted, and so she'd got no further.

At the Palace, she bowed and walked the best
she could, her mother and sister beside her,
plumped up like two fat pigeons.

They loved the attention. They flirted and smiled,
curtsied and danced. But not her. No, not her.

They flirted and smiled, curtsied and danced. But not her. No, not her.

At the far end of the grand hall the servant girl
sat, perched like a shimmering bird. Her throne
made of silver, her dress spun in gold. Her mother
and sister bowed to the servant girl like obedient
children.

But she couldn't. In front of everyone — the
guards, the ladies-in-waiting, the King and the
Queen — she heard herself say, 'I cut off my toe.'

'Why?' asked the servant girl.

But she could only shake her head and cry.

Her mother bundled her up in the carriage,
her face cracking in thunder.

'I swear I'll kill you, you rat. Don't you know
the servant girl will soon be Queen!'

Her sister shook her, snarling 'You will not ruin
me, sister dear, you will not ruin me.'

When she got home she buried her head in the
hole, into her feathery kingdom. She prayed
to the magic woman to come and take her away.
Just like the servant girl.

In the morning, her mother took the needle and
thread and sewed her daughter's lips together.
Then she shook her by the shoulders, hissing
'No words now for you, my lass. You shall be
our servant girl.'

Her sister hitched up her skirts and danced.

Her mother clapped and together they twirled, shouting 'Fetch the wine from the cellar, servant girl, fetch the wine.' Then they circled her, chanting 'Servant, girl, servant girl,' until she could bear it no longer. She crawled down the stairs, bought back the wine. Her mother and sister drunk it.

The following week was the servant girl's wedding. She went, with her mother and sister. She wore a deep purple lipstick that covered her stitches. She did not limp.

When they got back, her mother got rid of the second servant girl. It was now she who would scrub the stair, bake the bread, stir the stew. It was now she who would beat the carpets, turn the beds, wash the floors. She took to sleeping in the grate, amongst the ashes, down in the kitchen. One by one, her words shrivelled up inside her. Then they died.

Her mother and sister barked orders. 'Get my shawl, servant girl. Pour my bath, servant girl. Chop the wood, servant girl.' Over time she grew to like being silent. It comforted her, strangely.

She thought of the servant girl, Cinder, in the Palace. She wondered if she missed doing things. Cinder would have servants. They would brush her hair, dress her in gold.

And she wondered if Cinder would take her revenge. Like a dog off a leash, barking orders.

Snarling if the soup was too cold, the water too
hot, the sun too bright, the day too long.
Would she make people scurry, make people weep
as she had done?

Then she remembered. A time of long ago when
she was a little girl, Cinder had come into the
room, carrying a bucket. She had run up to her,
calling, 'Sister? Dear sister?' and wrapped her
arms around her.

Her mother, horrified, grabbed her, saying
'No, no, your sister is dead! Cinder is just the
servant girl. Do you understand? She is just the
servant girl.' And her mother had shaken her until
she had promised that she'd never call the servant
girl sister again. And then, through her tears,
she'd smiled for her mother.

That night, the sister of Cinder slept in the grate,
her tears wet and then dried by the warmth of the
little fire.

Forgive me, dear sister, forgive me.

As she fell asleep, she heard a mouse gnawing on
the dresser.

I'll catch it in the morning.

When she woke a man was making porridge by the
fire. His hair flowed over his shoulders,
like a golden waterfall. Soft, whispery fur ran
down his neck.

She wore a deep purple lipstick that covered her stitches.

His shirt was of fine woven wool that glistened silver in the light. He smelt of sugar.

Gently, he stirred the pot with a large wooden spoon. So intent he was, on his task, that she wondered if he knew she was there. Just as she thought this, he turned to her. His nose twitched. But the movement was so slight, so quick, she wondered if she had imagined it. She could hear the fire in the grate, crackle, crackle.

'Sit,' he said. She sat on the chair.

On the table rested a bowl, spoon and a pair of scissors. He pulled a stool towards her and sat close by, quietly breathing. His eyes were small and black. They twinkled like a night sky. How still he sat, in her little kitchen.

He took the scissors from the table. He lifted her face to his and then he cut, one by one, the blue-black stitches.

'Eat,' he said.

He served her two spoonfuls of the rich, honeyed porridge. How good it was. She filled her belly right, right up. When she was done, she put the spoon down and looked to him. She couldn't help herself. She smiled.

How beautifully strange it was! To feel a smile upon her face. One without malevolence, or sarcasm. One that filled her up, like the porridge.

Then again, she remembered. It was the day the
Prince had come, with his footmen and his guards.
How they had flustered, the three women. Herself,
her sister, her mother. How they had pranced about
in the parlour, like little geese, honking. The glass
slipper sitting on its velvet cushion in the centre of
the room. The grand prize.

Her sister had puffed and panted as she tried to
put the slipper on, her foot changing colour to
deep purple. 'The slipper fits,' she'd cried out.
'See dear Prince, how I dance?' She'd got up,
twirled about and then fell over.

Her mother had declined the offer of trying,
feigning a false modesty that even the daughters
had found hard to bear.

'Oh, I couldn't possibly, dear Prince, but how
flattering to be asked.' Then, when he'd turned,
she'd grabbed the slipper and tried to put it on and
the guards had to be called to get it off her.

Then a great stillness had fallen upon the room.
Standing, in the doorway, was the plain servant
girl. It was the way she stood, commanding a
presence so that they all had turned: herself, her
mother and sister, the Prince and his servants.

Then she had walked across the great carpet,
not waiting for an order, taking each step towards
them as if it were her right, a plain servant girl, to
be there amongst royalty. The glass slipper shone

bright upon its cushion as if it were calling for her to come, calling for her to come to complete it.

Cinder, the servant girl, covered in ash, put on the slipper as if she was putting on a plain, everyday shoe. It slid onto her foot like a second skin, all shimmering.

Then Cinder had smiled and her sister remembered how the room felt like the ceiling had opened and let the sun plummet into it, along with all the stars and moons, all the coloured rainbows. Cinder was the light itself, and they had become strange and broken planets, orbiting around her. Basking in her divine light. Stripped bare, made whole, forgiven.

The mouse man, the maker of porridge, watched Cinder's sister in the warm firelight. She felt herself falling into him, as if he were a deep and dark well and she surrendered in the falling.

Something was shifting inside her. Something so deep and hidden, something that she could barely name, was breaking free.

Their faces flickered to one another in the firelight.

Say my name. Say my name.

But she didn't utter a word. It was the thought of it that possessed her. How she yearned for her name to be spoken in that dark, damp, rotten little kitchen.

Say my name. Say my name.

The mouse man lifted his arms with such grace it

took her breath away. He cupped her face with his fine, long fingered hands. Their faces were so close, almost touching.

'Louisa,' he whispered. 'Louisa.'

And the walls came tumbling down. No longer was she sitting in a cold little kitchen but on high, in a mountain meadow. Long, lush, green grass lay all around her. Everywhere were snow-capped peaks and the air was full of blossom. Gently falling at her feet, on her face, in her hair. She could smell it on the breeze. The sweetness of it and the light touch of it was such a soft caress that it got her quietly weeping. So exquisite, so unexpected, so divine.

'Louisa,' she nodded, through her tears. 'Louisa.'

The mouse man and Louisa together bent their heads, their crowns lightly touching. For they were the King and Queen of a vast and glorious kingdom.

'Bring me my breakfast! Bring me my breakfast!' Her mother's voice tumbled towards her, bringing her back to her earth-bound kitchen.

The King and the Queen smiled at one another. Then the mouse man disappeared.

The day passed. Louisa made the beds, stirred the stew, washed the floors. She brushed her mother's hair, polished her sister's shoes, gave the cat its milk and walked the dog.

That night, down in the kitchen, Louisa heard a

mouse gnawing on the dresser. She smiled. She hung up her apron. On the hook above the fireplace.

Louisa put on a sturdy pair of boots, the ones that were kept by the back kitchen door. The road ahead was rough and winding. She knew they would serve her well.

In her bedroom Louisa packed a small, carpet bag. She took a feather from her kingdom and tucked it under her shirt. For good luck. She kissed her mother and sister as they lay sleeping. She crossed the long hall and opened the front door. She went out.

With a quiet click of the lock, the door closed tight behind her.

She went out. With a quiet click of the lock, the door closed tight behind her.

The Cubs

e puts his head in the oven.

Scattered bones. Burnt flesh.

He pulls his head out. He's dusty with all the ash.
Eyes big, like saucers.

'Tell me again' he says.

'I pushed her in, like that. Now she's dead.'

He's all roly-poly. It doesn't stop him. He goes
waddling out of that house as quick as he can.
Running a waddle round that icing-sugared house.
Shouting and yelling with glee.

'Clever sister! Clever, clever sister!'

Well he's puffing himself out with all his shouting
and waddling so he's plopping himself down.

Then he's weeping.

She's weeping too. Then they're laughing and
shouting because they can't believe it's all ended.

They stare at one other. She's as thin as a rake
and he's a humpty dumpty.

That night they curl up, giggling, in her little bed.
The bed breaks when he hops in. They don't care
because they're together again at last. Sleeping,
until the new dawn breaks.

'We must burn the house,' he says. 'Burn it
to the ground.' His bottom lip is trembling.

'I'll take a piece of the verandah,' she says.
'Some of the sill and the flint for our journey.'

She's seeing how he's changed. It's not just the
roly poly. He's been locked up in a cage
and he's gone a little strange.

I've gone strange too, she thinks, looking at her scarecrow
arms and the blue veins underneath her skin.
She's glad there's no mirror in the house.

They pack their few belongings.
They set the chickens free. They milk the goat.
Then they decide to take it with them.
On a little lead.

He sets fire to the house. It sizzles and pops.
The air is thick with smoke.
Burning sugar.

All three set out. Brother. Sister. Goat.
Into the woods. They're walking and walking.

From time to time he's lagging.

Turning, she sees him dropping something along
the path . . . 'What are you doing?'

He's looking sheepish. 'I found these.'

From out of his pocket he's taking out precious
stones. Diamonds, sapphires, rubies, emeralds.

'I found them upstairs, tucking under the nook.'

His bottom lip is trembling again. He's leaving a
trail, like last time. He's hoping there's someone
out there, looking for them.

That night they sleep together, next to the goat.
They tell each other stories. He tells her that he
was missing her so much that he named a little
sparrow after her that was nesting in the tree.
She pats his roly poly.

She doesn't say much. She won't tell him about
what went on in that sugar-coated house.
Instead she talks about what they might find on
their journey. Maybe they'll find something good.

'Like what?' he says, sitting up.
She can see his eyes shining with the thought of it.

'Maybe we'll find something better to what
we have found before.' She says that, carefully.
She can't think of anything good much.
Other than that the cannibal witch is dead.

The goat bleats. They all go to sleep.

In the morning they are thirsty. They milk the goat and munch on the verandah. It makes them sick now. They decide to burn those bits of house they've taken. In their little fire.

They take the flint, the goat and their few belongings. They're walking.

He's leaving a trail with his precious stones.

Up above, she's seeing the trees are getting taller. Even though they are in the thickest of woods, the light is soft. Birds jumping from bush to bush ahead of them. Their little blue tails catching in the green.

The further they walk, the lighter her step.

By mid-morning, they arrive at a stream. They both take off all their clothes, giggling.

Sitting in the water, he's washing off the ash and in between his roly poly.

She is washing her hair. She is crawling to him.

'Sister, sister.'
He's patting her. She didn't know she was screaming.

After some while her shaking ceases.

She is putting on fresh clothes. She is milking the goat.

They do not speak of it. Both of them knowing
now. Things are a little strange.

That night, she dreams of the cannibal witch.
She's beckoning to her. She has to go, because if
she doesn't the cannibal witch will eat her brother.
So she goes to her.

One foot in front of the other.
Inside she's shrinking.

One foot in front of the other. One foot.

The cannibal witch is stroking her hair.
Stroking her hair with her oiled-up fingers.
Clucking. Like a chicken.
Making her fetch the salt and pepper.

One foot in front of the other. One foot.

One foot in front of the other. One foot.

The cannibal witch is shaking the salt and pepper.
Shaking it in her hair. Rubbing, rubbing it
right in. Clucking, clucking all the while.

'Sister, sister.'

Waking at her brother's voice, she's crawling to
the water. Taking off all her clothes.
Scrubbing, scrubbing at her skin until . . .

It is raw. Glistening. In the moonlight.

The goat and the girl and the roly-poly boy
wake to the shouting of men's voices.
There's a roar of some wild beast.

Makes the trees bend.

All three tuck themselves right under the rock.
They don't move. All day and all night.

The following morning, she wakes.
The goat is lying next to her.

No brother.

'Hans? Hans?' she's whispering. 'Hans, Hans?'

She makes herself get out from down under.
The goat following. There's no sign of him.
Then she sees. Those precious little stones.
Dotted along one path. A trail. A trail.
That he has left for her.

Clever brother. Clever, clever brother.

She's walking all day, with the goat by her side.

Through the wood, through the shade,
through the shadow, through the light.
All the while those little stones reaching out.
Shining out. To her.

She wanders into a clearing.
Hans is sitting very, very still.

Before him lies a young bear cub. Laid out flat
against the stone. With a hunter's arrow shot.
Straight through his little heart.

Her brother is singing. Softly on the breeze.
It is a lullaby.

She closes her eyes. The song is some strange echo,
of some time, long ago. A mother's song,
for her baby. She's rocking that little cradle,
rocking, rocking.

And that little babe is ever so quiet.
Watching, in wonder, the mother sing.

The goat starts pulling on its lead.
Bleating, bleating.

Mother Bear comes in.
She is standing, as tall as a house. She roars.

Animals scatter. Birds fly. Trees bend.

When she wakes, Gretel has little idea where she is.
Up above, there is the goat, standing on the fork
of the upmost branch. High up in the tree.

There is a trickle of blood
 where Gretel's head has lain.

'Hans? Hans?'

Only the wood lark answers her.

'Hans? Hans?'

The goat bleats.

Gretel is wild now, a wild beast running through
the forest. Her little feet running like the wind.
Scarecrow arms, flapping, flapping.

Salt and pepper, salt and pepper.

No stones, no stones are calling out to her.

Salt and pepper, salt and pepper.

How she roars his name.
'Hans! Hans!'

Animals scatter. Birds fly. Trees bend.

She can smell the bear's lair as she turns over the
hill. Smells its rotting flesh. Her rage drives her
into a canyon of jagged stones. To the entrance
of a large cave.

How she roars, that scarecrow girl. How she roars.
The sound goes in, comes back out.
Then goes back in again.

Rocks fall from the top, crashing at her feet.
Earth trembling. Birds, screeching,
fleeing across the sky. Terror in their wings.

How she roars, that abandoned child.
Roars for her brother.

Mother Bear appears, towering above her. She's
holding Hans in her mouth. Placing him carefully at
Gretel's feet, she is lying down next to him.
She's looking at Gretel. Her eyes, full of sorrow.

Hans is waking. Milk oozing from his mouth.
Stretching out his roly poly. Then he's seeing her.
Seeing her cut feet, her jagged face.
Seeing her veins, pumping in her skin.

'Sorry Gretel,' he says.

Mother Bear tucks them in, under the folds
of her fur. Gretel on one side, Hans on the other.
Their little heads resting on her chest.

The goat is asleep, next to the small fire.

Hans is soft and sleepy.
'Sister, sister.'

She murmurs. Her belly is full of milk.

'This is better. To what we have found before.
So much better.' Her brother snuggles in to the folds
of fur. Mother Bear pats him.

Gretel watches the shadow of Mother Bear,
dancing on the cave wall.

Turning, Mother Bear looks down on her.
Gretel sees the world in her eyes.

The world in the water.

'There, there, Mother Bear, there, there.'

Mother Bear tenderly arranges her fur around her scarecrow daughter. She's gently rocking that little child. Until she's falling asleep.

The goat falls asleep too.

How they grow, those little children, living with their Mother Bear. How they grow, their arms stretched out. Dancing in the light.

Mother Bear is taking them to the river.
Full of salmon, thick and juicy. Hans lighting
the fire. Mother Bear flicking them the fish.
They fry them on the little rocks,
squealing in delight.

Mother Bear is lying under the water fall.
The water tumbling over her belly.
The children scampering up. Jumping off.
Sliding down her slippery fur.
Into the pool below.

Mother Bear is taking them to the tall trees.
The children, riding on her back. Mother Bear is standing. Reaching out, they are catching branches.
Climbing up farther. There is another world
to see on high.

At night, in the cave they tell stories.

Mother Bear tucks them in, under the folds of her fur. Gretel on one side, Hans on the other.

Drawing them on the wall. The little sparrow, Gretel. The sugar-coated house. The iron cage. Their father and his wife. They draw what they remember.

Gretel watches her brother change. His roly poly dripping off him. Legs growing, strong and supple. She too is changing.

One night Hans is sleeping. The goat is sleeping, too. Gretel is warm, tucked in. Mother Bear is singing to her. In a growling kind of way.

The little fire is dancing before them.

Gretel is watching it, watching it.
How that fire dances.

Gretel can feel the spell breaking inside her.

'Mother Bear, Mother Bear,' she's whispering.

Mother Bear falling silent, looking down on her.
Gretel feeling her beating heart, softly on her ear.

Gretel tells Mother Bear. All of what went on.
In that sugar-coated house.

In the darkness, in the nooks, in the crannies that brave little girl finds those dirty, shameful stories. Stuffed under the carpet they are, stuffed in the cracks of the floorboards. Out, out they come from little Gretel's mouth. Out, out into that flickering cave light. For all the world to see.

Salt and Pepper, salt and Pepper.
Clucking all the while.
Salt and pepper, salt and pepper.

Oiled up fingers.

Out, out the words fly out into the vastness of
that cave. Gretel feels the power seeping through her.
The power of the spoken word.
The power of her story.

Mother Bear is rocking that little child, rocking
in her cradle. Until she can speak no more.
The spell that was cast, has been broken.
The cannibal witch is dead.

Mother Bear is making them coats. For the winter.
A thick deer's hide for Hans. Another for Gretel.
And a coat made of rabbits for the goat.

Mother Bear is sleeping for the winter.
Hans, Gretel and the goat singing to her as
she's dreaming. Scampering around and over her.
Tucking themselves into her fur at night.

During the day they fish. At the hole Mother Bear
has dug for them. Building a little fire on the ice.
Sitting with their poles. Brother, sister and the
goat beside. They have become good hunters.

One day, in the summer, a man wanders by.
Into the canyon of jagged stones. Gretel can see
he is lost. He's dragging a broken heart behind,
on a little string.

'I am looking for my children,' he is saying.
'I deserted them long ago. I have something to give
you. If you can help me.'

Out of his pocket he's taking out precious stones.
Diamonds, sapphires, rubies, emeralds.
Letting them fall to the ground.

'Such riches. Take them, if you can help me.'

Gretel and Hans stand before that lost,
broken man. Knowing who he is.
Seeing his withered heart, tied with string.

'Come into our cave,' Hans says.

The man follows them. Into Mother Bear's cave.

Rocks tumble. Animals scatter. Birds fly.

Trees bend.

Knowing who he is. Seeing his withered heart, tied with string.

*T*Behind the *T*apestry

From the tower window, she's watching
her mother leaving. Knowing she will turn
when she gets to the first oak tree.

Sure enough, just as she's passing the oak,
she's turning. Waving.

She is walking to the stream now . . . a little farther.
Rapunzel knowing she'll call out
when she crosses at the first stone.

'Till tomorrow, daughter, till tomorrow.'

Now her mother is in the woods. Rapunzel will wait by
the window until she sees her, coming out on the far
side. At this point, her mother is almost unrecognisable.

There she is. Her mother. Beyond the wood
and far away. Walking, walking. No turning back now.
No waving, no calling out. Lost in her own thoughts.
Perhaps thinking of her daughter.
Perhaps thinking of her supper.
Perhaps thinking of tomorrow when she returns.

There. Her mother is gone. Rapunzel is clapping her hands in glee. The whole world is waiting for her. Outside that little window.

She's a clever girl. She's taking out that long, long hair and tying its end to the hook above the window. Now she's crawling out, and it's that sweet, sweet moment of nothingness.

Just as she's going over the ledge.

Down, down, the girl is slowly tumbling.
All the way, her hair, unravelling.
All the way, she's turning and twisting.
All the way to the ground.

She's looking up. Her hair stretching out
from up above. Safe and secure. For her return.

Oh, she's clever this girl. She unpins the thickness of the braid. Her mother thinks her hair is just this long. But this is her daughter's sweet, sweet secret.

Stretched out, her braid is three miles long and it can take her in any direction. From the north, to the south, the east and west. She can go a-wandering.

To the east, she knows the meadow is full of larkspur.
To the west, there are the crops of golden corn.
To the south, there is the stream and the wood beyond, but it is to the north she turns.
She has been dreaming of it.

She's skipping. The grass is tickling her feet.
The sun is warm. She feels the braid unravelling behind her. Feels its weight lifting at every step.

To the south, there is the stream and the wood beyond, but it is to the north she turns.

She's skipping and waiting for the moment.
And skipping a bit more.

There! It's the gentle tug. Her head pulling back,
ever so slightly. She loves this moment.
The turning around.

Seeing her hair stretching out. Reaching back,
following the path she has taken. Way, way back,
three miles back. To the tower. Far away.

To the north, she can see the sea.
Pulling up at the port, with their big white sails,
are the boats. And the tiny men, scurrying
beneath. Carrying their cargo.

One day she'll go there. She'll walk down the hill
before her, over the next rise, and then down into
the town. But not yet. Not quite yet.

Stepping back a little so her head can turn,
she's facing west. Watching the sun disappear,
in golden crimson. And Rapunzel is seeing how
beautiful the world is.

Now she's thinking of her supper. Waiting on the
tower table. Freshly picked grapes, milk and sugar
cake. Cold meat and bread. She is hungry.

Rapunzel is singing as she's walking back.
Braiding and looping her hair. She's imagining
how it will be when it's all gone.
When she is free of the weight of it.
Free of the pull on her neck.
Free of the ties that bind her to her mother.

She's climbing. Arms strong. Legs supple.
Up, up, back through the little window.
Into her tower.

She's eating her supper. The grapes are sweet.
The bread freshly baked. She's thinking of the tall
ships that she has seen. She has gathered many secrets.

The day she went a-wandering and met the
shepherd boy. Him moving his rough hands over her.
Gently, gently. How she cried out, in pleasure.

Or the day she went swimming with the girl.
Right down there in the stream. Naked they were,
their bodies entwined. A meeting of her own kind,
in another.

Secrets and more secrets she has gathered.
Hidden in the blue-shelled box. Behind the tapestry.

Daffodil bulbs. Acorns. Smooth pebbles from the
stream. A broken cow bell. Sometimes, when she is
waiting for her mother, she will take out the box.
She will look at them.

'Rapunzel, Rapunzel, let down your hair.'

'Coming, Mother,' she'll call out. Quickly, she'll
gather her things. Place them in the box. Hide them
behind the tapestry. She loves those moments.
The moments of the hiding.

Every day, her mother comes. They sit, talking in the
tower. Sometimes they play games. Sometimes they

look out the window. Rapunzel feels it pains her
mother. To look outside. Pains her, yet . . .
enchants her. Her mother is a confusion to her.

On the seventh day of that week, her mother does
not come. Rapunzel eats the left-overs of her
supper from the night before. She decides not to
go out. She sleeps well.

The following morning, she is at the window.
Looking for her mother. Looking for the figure
beyond the woods. Waiting for the moment of
recognition.

There is only deer. Grazing near the stream.
She eats the crumbs from the table. Again, she
decides not to go out. She does not sleep well.

The following morning, she is again at the window.
Someone is emerging from the woods.
It is the shepherd boy. He waves to her.

All that day, Rapunzel waits. That night she
dreams of breathlessness. She wakes to the sounds
of birds calling. Knowing she must go out now.
Out and look. For her mother.

There is no moment of sweet, sweet nothingness
as she's going over the ledge. Only dread.

Turning south she goes. Past the oak, she's turning
around. Her hair stretching back. A golden path.
To the window of the tower.
The sight gives her no pleasure.

She arrives at the stream and crosses at the first stepping stone. Now she is walking through the wood. Her hair weaving in and out of the trees as she's following the turning of the path. She's barely out of the woods when there's the tug. Her head pulling back. She can go no farther.

There is a little rock. She sits upon it. She waits. On the rock. For her mother to come.

The shepherd boy wanders by. And the girl she swam with. They are holding hands.
They see her and come over.

'What are you doing?'

'I'm waiting for my mother. It's been three days now and she has not come.'

'You must go to her village.'

'But I can't. My hair, my hair. It's not long enough.'
She's weeping now.

The shepherd boy is kind. 'In the meadow there is a sickle. I can fetch it. We can cut your hair. So that you can go to your mother's village.'

The girl is holding her now. Rocking her a little.
The shepherd boy goes and gets the sickle.
He and the girl cut off Rapunzel's hair.

'There, there. Now you can look for your mother. We can come with you.'

But she shakes her head. Angry all of a sudden.
'I want to go alone.'

She gets up and she's walking. She's thinking if
she were watching from the tower window,
she'd be a distant figure at this point.
Someone disappearing. Almost gone.

The wind is dancing at her neck. Her hair is jagged.
Rapunzel's often wondered at this moment.
How it would feel. She'd thought she'd feel
set loose and fancy free.

She'd imagined that one day she'd go to her box
and take out the scissors that she had found.
To her mother's horror, she'd cut it all off, the hair
on her head. It would fall to the ground at their feet.
And there would be this moment. Of a long
and great silence. There between them.
Mother. Daughter. Standing in the tower room.
By the window.

As she's going to her mother's village, Rapunzel's
realising she wants it all back. The hair on her head.
The pull on her neck. The burden.

You see, the moment of severance was meant to be
of her choosing. But that's not how it's played out.

It's been six years since her mother dragged her
to the tower. Rapunzel is surprised at how easily she's
finding her way back. To the high-walled house.

Villagers pass by her in the market square.
Some recognise her. She wonders why she wasn't
fetched. But she's knowing how her mother was both
revered and feared. People would have been wary.

At the house gate, there are candles burning.
This is the moment for sure. The daughter is
knowing what she has felt these three days passed.
Her mother is dead.

In the kitchen, her mother is laid out. In a coffin
on the flagstone table. Eyes closed. Mouth open.
Flowers have been laid all around. Her mother looks
peaceful. And her daughter gazes at her.
In both shock and wonder. Such a powerful figure.
Now she lies so still. Quiet.

That night, Rapunzel sleeps in her old bed.
In the middle of the night she is woken.
By the sounds of whisperings in the kitchen.

Looking through the key hole, Rapunzel sees an
old couple that are familiar to her. Then she remembers.
The neighbours. The man now stooped, his wife
more so. They have bought their little wheelbarrow
in from their garden.

By candlelight, the man is carefully placing spadefuls
of earth on top of her mother. From the neck down
to her best shoe. He's emptying little piles of dirt,
following the hushed instructions of his wife.

Then together they plant lettuces.
Batavian, Butterhead, Salanova, Rapunzel.
Now his wife is lifting up the watering can.
Carefully watering them in. Afterwards they sit.
Whispering to one another in the candlelight.
Rapunzel can't make out if they are cursing

or praying until the moment the wife gets up and spits on her mother's face. Then they wheel the barrow out of the kitchen, making sure no dirt has fallen to the floor. Quietly closing the door behind.

Rapunzel, waking in the morning, thinks she must have dreamt it. But wandering into the kitchen, she sees her mother, laid out in her box on the flagstone table. With a garden of lettuces planted on her, all in little rows.

And the daughter is thinking that her mother had secrets too.

That afternoon, her mother is buried. It is a small gathering. The neighbours do not come. Some words are spoken. But not many. Rapunzel can feel people's wariness.

After the burial, Rapunzel goes back to the high-walled house. She wanders the rooms and the garden. She will not stay for long. She sleeps one more night in her mother's house.

In the morning, she leaves the key hidden in the crook of the mulberry tree. By the side of the back door. In a little tin. She has taken her mother's silken scarf and wrapped it around her neck to keep it warm. She has taken some silver pieces from behind the brick in the fireplace. Some secrets she knows.

As she's walking back through the town, she passes the neighbours the other way. She nods at them, a little wary.

'Fine day,' says the stooped man and tips his cap. His
wife says nothing. But Rapunzel can feel her gaze.

'Yes,' says Rapunzel. His wife is still gazing.
It is not the look of a neighbour.

'Come, dear,' he says and he gently takes his wife's arm.

'No,' she says. 'Let us stop. Just for a moment.'

So the three of them stop in the road. The man,
with his hand on his wife's arm, just placed so lightly.
His wife, gazing at the girl.

There they wait. Rapunzel not knowing why
she can't move, but there it is.

'Come dear,' he says again after a time. And this time
his wife goes with him. As if she has drunk just a little
sip of something and that it is enough. For the time.

And the daughter is thinking that her mother had secrets too.

And so they walk away from one another.
Rapunzel to the market square.
The neighbours homeward-bound.

Back through the village, Rapunzel goes out into the
countryside. Through the woods and out the other side.
Crossing at the stream with a hop, skip and a jump
on the stepping stones.

Ahead is the tower with its wisps of hair
billowing from the window. But it is to the north
Rapunzel turns. As she has been dreaming of it.

With the grass under her feet. She's walking, walking.
And then she's running. Running, running.
Down the hill and over the rise.
Down into the town.

Crossing at the stream with a hop, skip and a jump on the stepping stones.

Things to be Getting on with

When she became God, it was not long before the fisherman's wife had it out with the flounder.

'I know you'll be disappointed about me being a woman and all, but just get over it,' she said. 'Now go back to your sea. I won't be bothering you again.'

With that, she hitched up her dress, sat down in the boat, and rowed back to shore. She trudged her way back up the beach.

Not once did she look behind her.

Then she talked sternly to her husband.

'You're going to be helping out a bit more around the house,' she said. 'Now that I'm God, I've got a bit on my plate. I certainly don't want to be coming home to your dishes!'

The fisherman didn't dare argue with his God wife. He pulled up his sleeves. Started helping around the house.

It was no palace for sure. More of a pigsty.

The boards were bare. It was draughty and cold. The windows cracked. The goats and the pigs slept at the back with the donkey. In the kitchen, there were two families of mice, seven rats, and a dozen cats and kittens. With more on the way.

It was true. Things had got away from them.

'What will you be doing? Now that you're God?' the fisherman asked his God wife.

'I'll think of something,' she said, and blew out the candle.

She started snoring.

The fisherman, in his mind, went through all that had happened thus far. It started one week ago.

Catching that flounder.
Out there in his boat.

'Don't be eating me now,' it had said. 'I haven't been well. I wouldn't want to pass it on to you.'

He'd never been talked to by a fish.

When he told his wife, she'd cuffed him and said that he had to go back in the morning.

'It's a talking fish, you silly man. It's full of magic. And since you let it go, it's owing us. Tell that flounder I want a good house. One that doesn't leak.

With a step at the front door. So I can wipe my
boots on it.'

So the fisherman had reluctantly rowed back the
following morning. Into the little bay.

Although the flounder was annoyed by the
fishwife's demands, she got what she wanted.
A nice little house, with a nice picket fence.
The fisherman thought all was well.

But then his wife sent him back again.

She wanted a bigger house and then, after that,
a palace.

Then she wanted to be King, then Emperor.

Sitting on her Emperor throne, she wanted to
be Pope.

The fisherman dragged his feet down to the shore.
Took out the boat once more.

Each time the fisherman asked, the flounder
grew angrier. The sea darker and darker.
The waves bigger and bigger.

Then the fisherman refused to go out at all.

But the wife, now Pope, wanted to become God.

Well, the fisherman shook his head and his feet did
not move. So his Pope wife cuffed him and said,
'I'll just do it myself.'

And so he watched her. From the balcony of the Pope's palace. Along with all the Cardinals and Bishops. Priests and altar boys.

They all looked terrified.

There she was. Trudging down to the shore. In her Pope's outfit. It wasn't easy. Her golden hat kept falling off her head. Her flowing robes kept twisting round her legs. But she persisted.

A terrible storm was breaking. Taking out the boat, she rowed to the middle of the bay.

The fisherman could see, even from this distance, that the flounder had surfaced. The waves were crashing about. Lightning in the sky. Thunder cracking. It felt as if the world were ending.

His Pope wife was standing in the boat. Shouting and waving her arms about. The flounder waving his fins and shouting back.

They seemed to go on for all eternity.

But then, gradually, after a long time, the sea calmed. The thunder stopped. The fisherman could faintly hear his Pope wife and the flounder. But not their words, though they were in lively conversation. The flounder had laughed and his wife had laughed. Then it seemed to be all over.

His wife sat down in the boat and began rowing back. With every stroke of the oar the Pope's palace sunk into the sand. The Cardinals and Bishops,

Priests and altar boys sunk into the sand as well.
They were terrified.

The fisherman could see his wife's golden robes
disintergrate upon her. Even his own fine,
embroided outfit disappeared.

By the time the fisherman's wife struck the shore
she was back in her rags, he back in his, and the
Pope's palace had become their hovel once again.

He went out to meet her as she was dragging the
boat up on the beach.

His God wife nods at him. 'That went well,'
she grunts. Then she hitches up her filthy skirt
and wanders back into their home.

His God wife nods at him. 'That went well,' she grunts.

Everything had changed. Nothing had changed.

Well, he wasn't sure.

There she was. His God wife, now sleeping.
Snoring her head off as always.

'We could do with some chickens,' says his God
wife in the morning. And sure enough, there was a
cluck, cluck, cluck at the door.

Opening it, he sees three chickens and a rooster.
Sitting on the front step.

'I kept the step,' his wife says, winking.

The three chickens and the rooster wander in.
They sit upon the table. Sure enough,
three eggs are laid.

He and his wife eat them scrambled.

'What will you be doing?' asks the fisherman.
'Now that you are God?' But he's tentative as he
asks this because he has no idea what is going on.

She says 'I'll think of something.'

By mid-morning, she's scrubbing the step and the
windows. She says to him, 'Take the pigs outside,
with the donkey and the goats. Take them down
to the beach for a while. I want to clean their
mangers.'

Well, he looks alarmed. He can see himself

running all over the beach, chasing piglets and such like. His God wife is watching him.

She fixes him a stare and says,
'Don't you be forgetting who I am.'

So he's taking all the animals down to the beach.

When he gets there, the sun is shining and there's a lovely breeze. It is all very pleasant. The pigs wandering around, but not too far. The piglets staying close to their mothers. The goats chewing tussock. The donkey sleeping.

When he comes back, they all follow him in little rows. First the pigs and their babes, then the goats and the donkey. They all weave through the dunes, and when they get to the front step all the animals stop. They wipe their little feet upon it. Then they go inside.

Well, that God wife has been busy. The mangers scrubbed and cleaned, fresh straw lain. The sweet smell of linseed fills the air.

Through the little kitchen, the animals go.
Right on their tippy toes. So as not to leave a mess.
Out the back, into their mangers.

Fresh water in buckets, meal and oat cakes greet them. They bray and squeal in delight.

His God wife is asleep near the fire, snoring.

He can see her hands are red raw.

From all the scrubbing she's done.

From the shelf above the sink he takes down a small jar. He undoes the lid. He scoops a little of the pig fat out of it. Taking his God wife's hand he gently rubs some into her skin.

His God wife wakes and looks at him. In her eyes he is seeing an endless night sky, full of shooting stars.

Smiling at him, ever so quietly, she says,
'I've had a good day being God.'

'You carry it well,' the fisherman whispers.
'Upon your shoulders.' He kisses her on her cheek.

They snuggle in together and watch the fire burning. They reminisce. When they first met, their first kiss, their first child. The death of their second. The joy of their third.

'It is a good life,' she says, patting his arm.
Then she goes to bed. And starts snoring.

In the morning, the fisherman wakes. His God-wife is putting on her boots and wearing a clean skirt, nicely patched and ironed. There's her pretty silver earrings in her ears, her green scarf wrapping round her shoulders.

'Where are you going?' he asks his God wife.

'Out,' she says. 'There's things to be done. I'll be back by the end of the week. Finish off what I've started, dear husband.' Then she looks at him, making sure he's understands.

Placed on the freshly scrubbed kitchen bench there's a list she's written on a piece of paper. She puts this in her pocket and takes her coat that hangs by the back door. She blows a kiss as she's going out.

He watches her from the window.

She takes the road. He watches her until she has gone over the small hill. He wonders what she's up to.

The goats, pigs and the donkey wait for him. Then they tippy-toe through the kitchen and down into the dunes, wandering around the beach in the warm sun. Since they're so well behaved, he has time to fix his cray pots. Then he oils the boat and plugs the leak that's been bothering him for years.

Then the animals all line up, and wait for him again. Then they all walk back to the tumble-down cottage, tucked up there in the dunes. They all wipe their feet on the front step, tippy-toe through the kitchen and back into their mangers.

The fisherman scatches his head.

Nothing has changed. Everything has changed. He wonders what his wife is up to.

In the middle of the night he is woken by heavy rain. He places little buckets all around. To catch the drips. The following day he sets to on the roof,

patching and repairing the leaks that have been
bothering him for years.

That night, the rains come again but this time
the house is snug and the animals in their mangers
are dry.

The following morning, he decides he doesn't want
the rats and the mice living in the kitchen anymore.
He makes them some little houses. Out of thrush.
He hangs them above, where the donkey lives.
The rats and the mice move out of the kitchen and
into their little houses.

The fisherman sets to and scrubs down all the
benches, cleans out the cupboards, airs the
linen and does four loads of washing. Each day the

In his little boat. He sets his pots. Amongst the sea garden.

animals tippy-toe through the kitchen, down to the beach. He doesn't need to go with them anymore.

He wonders what his wife is up to.

On the fourth day, the sea turns olive green. He can see it's full of plants. Fish, seals and birds are feasting on it. There's a crispness in the air he's never felt before.

He rows out. Into the bay. In his little boat. He sets his pots. Amongst the sea garden.

Nothing has changed. Everything is changing.

He wonders what his wife is up to.

That night it rains again, and he goes and stands in it. It feels like silk. Silk running down and through him. Then all the animals come out of the house. The donkey, goats, pigs and their piglets. The rats and mice, cats and kittens.

Together they all stand with him in the silken rain. They are silent and still. They can feel it too. How good it is.

In the morning, the sky is streaked in crimson and gold. It stays like this all day. Even though the sun has risen and moves through the sky and then beds down again, on the other side.

He rows out into the bay. He can see his pots. They are filled with the biggest bounty.

Then he rows out farther. There's that crispness in the air. It smells so sweet. As if it's the first day of spring. Everything feels new. He rows and rows. Right down there, in the depths below, he can see thick forests of kelp, teaming with fish that he has never seen before. In all his years as a fisherman.

Everything has changed. Nothing has changed.

He rows back to shore. He hopes his wife is home soon.

She's asleep in the chair. He takes her tattered shoes off. Her feet are blistered and raw. In her hands glass shards have pricked her palms. Small cuts are festering.

On her right cheek there is heavy bruising.

Her clothes are filthy.

He is filled with such love for her. He is bursting.

He takes down the freshly scrubbed pot. Fills it with water to heat. He takes a cake of soap from the drying rack.

He fetches clean clothes for his wife. Newly washed and patched whilst she was away.

He gently wakes her and washes her. Undressing her by the fire. He washes her beautiful, old, exhausted body, the one that has borne him his children.

He is gently dressing her again.

One by one, he takes out the shards in her hands.

He washes her beautiful, old exhausted body, the one that has borne him his children.

Brushes her hair and feeds her the soup from the stove.

He carries her to their bed. She smiles at him.
Her eyes are full of dancing stars.

As she's sleeping, he takes some paper and makes a list. Of the things that still need doing around the house. A little path of pebbles to the well so that the mud can be kept out. Some flowers planted, just by the step, to greet them when they go in and out.

New blankets. He can trade some fish with the farmer next door. For some wool.

He gets into bed, next to his God wife.
Blows out the candle. She is snoring.

When he wakes she is looking at him.
She kisses him gently on his cheek.

'What will you be doing today?' he asks his God wife.

'I'll think of something,' she says.

The $\mathcal{M}$an in the dress

e arrives. Although he is lost.

It is still, as if just about to snow.
But the bulbs have burst, and there is a
wild, flowered carpet beneath his feet.

Underneath the far tree is a mound, covered in
moss. He tip-toes across. There's a small opening.
Crawling inside, he finds a young woman, very
pale, seemingly asleep. Her dress is light blue,
and there's a posy in her hand.

Because she is pretty and because he is bold,
he kisses her.

She wakes, looking at him. Her hair is black,
her skin white. He feels moved by the sight of her,
as if he's known her all along. He takes her hand,
leading her out into the wild, wild forest.

She wanders away. But her trail is easily followed.
He arrives at a tiny house, tucking under the roots
of an enormous tree. Inside, she is singing.

Then he lies and sleeps because he has travelled far.

Waking, there is a bowl of soup beside him.
Three pieces of freshly baked bread.

'Hello,' she says, smiling. He smiles back.

While he's been sleeping, she's been working.
There's a row of little clothes along the line.
The windows of the house are all a-gleaming.

He watches her walk to the well and wash her long
black hair. He wonders about her. Where she has
come from. Why she is living in such a tiny house.
She has to stoop to go in and stoop to go out.

He wonders about the little pairs of boots outside
the door. 'Where are the children?' he asks.

'Coming.'

He watches her shake out the carpet.

'Come.' She takes his hand. Stooping,
he goes inside that tiny house.

Seven little beds lie along one wall. There are seven
cups, seven bowls, seven spoons and saucers.

In the corner is a bigger bed. She lies down upon it.

'I am tired. We will sleep, just as children,
with your arm across me so.'

She turns her back and places his arm over her.
He nestles into her neck. She smells of apples.
Remembering his mother, he cries a little.

'Shhh, shhh.'

She turns her back and places his arm over her. He nestles into her neck.

When he wakes, she is sitting on the bed,
watching him. It gives him some kind of feeling,
deep inside.

He asks. 'Do you know me?'

She says nothing. Noticing the red of her lips,
he follows her outside, to where the sun is shining.

She is singing again. All the little birds come and
fly around her, like flying ribbons for her long
black hair. Lizards come out from their little holes.
Snakes slither across the grass.

A herd of young deer stop to hear her.

And he knows he is seeing magic.
And he feels he is living in a spell.
Along with the little boots, the little beds,
the little cups and saucers,

That night, they sleep again as children.
In the morning, a strange fear rises up inside him.
He knows it is time to go.

'Take the path by the river and cross it further
downstream. You will see the tree with the stump
beside. Cross over there, the current is weak.
From there you will find your way back.'

From the hill, he knows she is watching him.
Wearing her light blue dress.

Taking the path by the river, he sees the tree with
the stump. Crossing there, the current is weak.

On the far shore, he finds a path which runs along
the river. He walks his way back.

His friends find the young man in a small
cove beside the water. He is wearing a tattered
dress, barely breathing, his skin blue and black.

How he has come to be there and the nature of
his clothing is a great mystery to both him and
everyone else. He is told he was a soldier,
left for dead on the battlefield. Yet he has no
memory of it. His memory is of the mossy mound
and the young woman in the light blue dress.

His friends throw a party. His parents weep,
for they feared him long dead. His Love, left
behind, had waited for him.

Soon he is married. His wife bears him
four children. He is a happy man.

That winter is bitterly cold, and a great sickness
falls upon the land. Many are dying. His wife falls
ill, then all his children. He nurses them.
He wipes his wife's brow, tries to feed his young
babe. They are all pale, thin, barely breathing.

And the memory of the young girl overshadows
him. As if her spirit has been with him all along.

'Where are the children?'
'Coming'

He remembers her shaking out the carpet.

It is the middle of the night. He is seized by terror.
Quietly getting up, he moves back all the furniture.
It makes no sense to him, why he is doing it.
Dragging the carpet out from his house.

It is windy, cold. Snow is falling. In that blizzard
he does his best. He shakes out the carpet.

Dragging it back inside, moving back the furniture,
lying in the bed blue with cold. He is ice.

Waking, his wife and four children are gathered
round him. They are weeping.

'Papa, Papa.'

Holding out his ice-blue hand, seeing the rose in
their cheeks. He knows they are all better.

In that blizzard he does his best. He shakes out the carpet.

'Papa, Papa.'

'Shhh, shhh.'

His wife wipes his brow. He is loving her so much.
He is a happy man.

Closing his eyes, he is flying across a river.

Come lie with me like children, for we are tired.

He is spinning himself into a fine thread, then
weaving himself into her hair, like a shiny ribbon.
Her dress is flying all around them.
She is the woman with the long black hair.

Upon waking, the man sees there are little
children all around him. One is weeping,
one is glum, and one is very thirsty.

'Where are my children?'

'We are your children and we are hungry.'

Shaking his head, confused, the man gets out
of bed. These are not his children.

Putting the pot on the stove, he has to stoop
everywhere because the roof is so low. All the
while, he is remembering his own family.

With all the stooping he is doing, he knows he's
in the dream now. He's in that tiny house tucking
under the great tree. And he's got a deep feeling.

Peeling seven carrots and seven onions,
he puts them into the pot.

Then he lays out seven cups, seven bowls,
seven spoons and saucers.

He stirs the soup. The little faces of the children
are watching. They are very, very quiet.

Putting the pot upon the table, he takes the large
spoon and serves them the soup.

'Where's the bread?' asks the glum one.

He is about to say he hasn't any. Then the
sweet smell of baking bread fills his nostrils.
Turning to the little oven, all the while
stooping his head, he opens the oven door.
He pulls out a lovely little loaf.

'That's better,' says the weepy one.

Slurping their soup, they chatter. Sitting on a
larger stool, the man is wondering what to do with
all the confusion in him. And then he sees the
dress. A light blue one. And he is wearing it.

Well, that man goes running out of that house,
almost knocking himself out on the low beam
above the doorway. Running to the top of the hill,
then running into the wild, wild wood and back
out again. Running around the great tree and then
running around the well. Hitching his skirt, he is
running around like a crazy rabbit.

The glum child comes walking up the hill.
'Why are you running?'

They are both on the top of the hill now.

The man in the dress is panting.
'I want to go home.'

'But you are home,' says the child.
'This is your home and we are your children.'

'No, no. I remember everything. My wife, my four
children, my parents though they are dead. I
remember my house and the land that sits around it.
I remember my friends.'

He moves his hands across the skirt and he can feel
the cotton in it. It's the cotton in his baby's cap
and his fingers are patting it down, patting it down.

Then all those little children come walking up
and stand all around him. They are ever so quietly
watching him.

Hitching his skirt, he is running around like a crazy rabbit.

'Where is your mother?' asks the man in the dress.

'Down by the river.'

'I'll be saying goodbye now.' Hitching his skirt,
the man in the dress goes walking. Down to the river.

As he's walking, he's thinking.

*I'll cross the river at the tree where the stump is
because the current is weak there.*

He's been so wrapped up in his thoughts that he
hasn't noticed the river is not as it was before.
By the time he arrives at the tree with the stump,
the current is wild. The river is swollen.
The farthest shore is a very faint sight in the distance.

The man in the dress sees how the water is pulling
things under. But he must go back. His wife and
children are on the other side. So he jumps in.

Well, his dress is blowing up all around him,
swirling in the froth and the foam. He's trying to
swim across, but now he's swallowing the water.

Just as he is thinking he is drowning,
a log passes by. He grabs onto it. It takes him across
to the far side of the river, into a little cove,
where the waves are gently lapping.

He stumbles onto the grass, his dress clinging to him,
his two feet squelching in their shoes.

He has to lie down. He feels very, very tired.

Waking from sleep, his dress is dry.

Standing, he looks across the river.
It is no longer swollen, angry. It is deep and still.
He can see the other side, closer to him this time.

And there she stands.
The woman in the light blue dress.
She is watching him.

He is moved by the sight of her.
The way the sunlight is catching in her hair.
And even from this distance, those red, red lips.

And he is seized by the power of another life,
in another world, beyond this shore.

In his mind he can see their home, where the roof
is so low he has to stoop and bend his head.
He can see his children gather round
to hear his stories.

He can see at night, reaching out.
Touching, caressing that long, black hair.

The man in the dress turns round.
Behind him is the path that he knows.
At his feet is the log that has carried him across.
It is gently nudging him, nudging him.
The water is quietly lapping.

Come lie with me like children for we are tired.

It is the blue of the dress shouting out against
the snow.

That is how they find him.
Lying on one side, curled up like a little child.
His hands tucked under his cheek,
as if he is praying.

He's wearing a tattered dress, its skirt splayed out,
like a flag. It is a heralding of his departure.
From this life.

As to the nature of his clothing, his friends do not
speak of it. Quietly removing the dress, they burn
it and dress him in borrowed clothes before
carrying his body back to his wife and home.

His wife thinks he had somehow stumbled out,
in the middle of the night, in a fever.

They must wait many months, until the earth
thaws. Then, in the spring he is buried.
They place him under a little mound of freshly dug
earth that smells sweet.

His children plant daffodils all around.

Watching from the fold

'Come to bed.'

'In a while.'

'Come to bed, dear heart.'

He blows out the candle. There's a lonely, empty cave beside him in their bed. She'll come when first light appears and sleep until mid morning. It's been like this for two weeks.

His wife is believing that one night, she will see, the maker of the miracles.

'Wake up, husband. Wake up.'

He follows her candlelight down the stairs.

'Look, husband, look.'

From behind the curtain, he sees two little elves, naked as new-born babies. They are stitching a new pair of boots. He watches them jump about, over the leather, under the leather, their little hands flying.

In-out go the stitches, in-out. How quickly the red
leather boots rise from the table.

'Tonight they show themselves,' his wife whispers.
'We have been blessed by the little people —
and look at them, with not a stitch between them!'

They watch them together, from behind the
tattered curtain.

The magic is in the workshop, but he can feel the
breathing of her, next to his skin. She smells of
cinnamon and nutmeg. He can't work out how that
can be because there's been no baking in the house
since the all-night vigils.

He sees how the silver of her hair catches the light,
as if a bolt of lightning has been struck right in it.

Soon, a second pair of boots rise from the table.
Then three pairs of slippers, a heavy man's belt and
two pairs of mittens.

The little people are all a-chattering, but when the
shoemaker sneezes they scamper off out the window,
quick as can be.

His wife is angry with him for sneezing.
Doesn't talk to him all day. Only when night falls
and they are sitting by the fire, does she speak.

'I'll be making them some clothes, husband, with
the finest velvet I can buy. What with the cold
weather coming.'

He only nods. Words will make it worse. He can feel

the worry in her. The worry that they've scared the little people off and that the days of wonder have all but ended.

In his workshop, he takes out two pieces of leather, his finest thread, and scissors.

He makes sure everything has been left exactly as before: the broom in the corner, the chair by the door, the curtain and the window just half open.

Upstairs, his wife is in bed.

'I thought it better to be keeping here tonight, husband. So that there can be no clatter.'

He nods again, yearning, dreading, for morning to come. By then, he dares to hope, he'll be able to do some talking. He blows out the candle.

Like two well worn spoons they snuggle into one another.

Like two well worn spoons they snuggle into one
another. He breathes her in, as he has always
breathed her in. At this moment, every night,
since they were newly weds.

They sleep till late. It is with trepidation that they
go down the stairs.

The broom is in the corner, the chair is by the
door. The curtain and window are half open.
And on the bench lay two pieces of leather, with
the thread and the scissors beside them.

'Oh, husband, what have you done? What have you
done?' And she sits on the stair and weeps.

He stands all alone, dry-mouthed.
The pit of his stomach churning.

He goes out to the woodshed.
Takes it out on the wood. The frustration he feels,
the devastation.

When he comes back, the house is empty.
He fears she has left him. But there's a scuffle on
the step and his wife appears,
carrying a little parcel.

'I've bought the velvet, as I said. I don't want
disturbing. You'll be getting your own supper.'
With that, she closes the door tight behind her.

He fries up some eggs. Offers them to his beloved.
She's intent on her task, barely hears him.
And again he notices the lightning in her hair.

He blows her a kiss, brave man that he is,
before he goes up to their bed.

In the morning she's still cutting and sewing.
She feels far away. He doesn't know how to
reach her.

He goes back to the shed in the cold morning light.
Takes it out on the wood.

'You might as well be getting on with it, husband.
There's the leather on the bench and the needle
and thread. No good chopping wood all day,'
she says through the door.

He makes some boots. Fine boots. With a little fur
at the peak and some nice stitching. He sells them
to the baker's wife. By nightfall, his stomach feels a
little better.

'Come to bed.'

'No.'

'Come to bed, dear heart.'

His wife watches him put the broom against the
wall, just so. The chair by the door, just so. The
curtain and the window just half open. She looks
worn and smooth. Her stiff fingers working the
velvet.

'Can I help?'

'No.'

He hesitates by the door. Then, brave man that he

is, he lights a second candle and places it carefully near the first, so that the light from the two illuminate her working.

He wants to carry her upstairs, over the well worn threshold, to their bed. He wants to sink into her and feel her sinking into him. That is the moment he lives for. Everyday of his life and forever more.

The cold cave awaits him. There's something stirring in him, something dark and sinister rising. He falls asleep. Thankfully it's forgotten.

In the morning, he tiptoes down the stairs, lights the fire, opens the workshop door. His wife is slumped over the bench, quietly snoring. Beside her lie two little night-blue suits, with lace collars and fine stitching. Next to them are two pairs of velvet shoes, stockings, scarves, mittens and caps.

His wife feels cold. He pulls the blanket down from the upstairs bed and places it over her shoulders. He makes the porridge, chops the wood, all the while thinking of his wife and her little, fine suits that she has made. He prays that it works, her plan, to lure them back. Back into this world. Those magic little people.

She's in bed. A fever is burning her. But she won't see the doctor. She'll take just three spoons of porridge and a sip of tea. She gives him strict instructions. He's to leave the clothes laid out so, with a candle burning.

He does everything she wants. Then, in the evening he checks the broom by the wall, the chair by the door, the window and the curtain.

He waits. Watches and waits.
Behind the tattered curtain.

He wakes. He is slumped in the corner. The curtain has been pulled back. He can hear soft, gentle whisperings. On the bench, the two little people sit, dressed in their fine, warm velvet. With their caps on their heads, the mittens on their hands, and the slippers and the stockings swinging.

He doesn't move, barely breathes.

On the bench is a vast array of the finest footwear he has seen. High riding boots, in night black leather. Court shoes in fine tapestries. Slippers, work boots, scarlet gloves, feathered hats. His workshop is full of it, full to overflowing.

What should he do? Should he speak?

They turn to him, the little people, as if they have known him there all along. Big eyes blinking.

There is a wonder between them all. The wonder of them, in their little blue suits, and the wonder of him in the corner.

He slowly stands. And they stand too. He takes a step towards them and they too take a step towards him. He stops because he's afraid they'll topple off

the bench. Then they run at him and jump, into the
void, and with a loud shout he's moved
forward and scooped them up in his hands
and they're laughing and he's laughing and they
scurry up his long, bony arms and nestle into his
neck, like two little door mice.

He can't quite believe it. He can feel their warmth
and the soft, smooth velvet against his skin.
He wants to show them to his wife. Show her that
her magic has worked. They have come back, the
little people, and all is as it was before, when life
became extraordinary.

Together they climb the stairs. He opens the door
to the bedroom. It's cold. The window is wide open.

On the bench is a vast array of the finest footwear he has seen.

He quickly shuts it, pulling the curtain back so the
sun can pour in.

His wife is a lump in the bed. He goes to her,
with the elves sitting on either side of his shoulders.
Perched like two tiny birds.

'Dear heart, dear heart.'

She doesn't stir. He gently pulls the covers back.
His heart freezes. His wife is a deep, dark shade of
purple, barely breathing.

The two little elves scamper down his arms and sit
on the bed cover, just where the sheet is folded back.
They watch his wife's sleeping face, filled with an awe
that frightens him.

They can understand what is happening and he can't,
although he fears it.

They sit and watch. Watch how the purple washes
through her.

He thinks he should fetch the doctor. But the thought
is fleeting. Arising in him is knowledge of an ancient
kind.

Be still! Keep vigil!

They watch her all day.
The two elves and the old man.

At night the elves want him to take them back to the
workshop. He carries them down in his outstretched
hands, like two offerings.

He sleeps. Next to his wife. She has become the cold cave. He breathes her into the pit of his chest. His dreams are lost and lonely.

When he wakes, he hears scuffles on the stair. The door is opening. Two fine slippers appear, beautifully stitched. They move across the floor, as if by magic. But the shoemaker knows the little people are behind them, pushing them along.

They wait for him to come. Come and lift them to the bed. With their little heads sunk into their tiny little chests, they are, he can hear, quietly weeping.

And in that moment he knows his wife will not be getting better.

And between them all they put the slippers on the shoemaker's wife as she lies dying.

She begins singing. The softest sound.
Like through a reed. A note, pure, sweet.

At first, the shoemaker thinks it's the wind at the door. He walks to the stair and cocks his head, just so. It sounds like it comes from beyond their cottage, from beyond their village.

From beyond the mountains that lie at the edge of the horizon.

Then he leans over his wife.
It is coming from her mouth.

'What is it my love? Does it pain you?'

His whisperings feel fake, hollow. A meagre, insignificant gesture in the presence of something of an infinite nature. He keeps quiet.

On his wife's chest, the elves sit, just on the fold. As she breathes, they rise up and down with the movement, as if on a gentle sea.

They watch her face, transfixed by the sound and the colour of her skin.

She is changing. Ebbing and flowing into deep shades of sea green. Small fish appear, swimming across her cheek, over the bridge of her nose, and then disappearing back into her hair. Schools and schools of little sparkling fish. Swimming over her, through her. She is a garden of the sea.

The elves, entranced, clap in delight. Their little clapping sounds fall into the sound that she is singing.

The shoemaker sits down. On the chair beside the bed. It is all too much for him.

When he wakes, the elves are curled up on his wife's chest, fast asleep. Again she has changed. Leaves are falling down in her now. In colours of burnt orange, amber. From the top of her head, down to the bottom of her feet, she has become a great forest in the fall.

She is still breathing. There is the softest of sounds in the air.

He goes down to the kitchen and makes some
porridge, stoking up the fire from the last
of the wood.

In his grief, the thought of chopping gives him
comfort. He takes the axe to the woodshed.

Inside it smells sweet. He takes pleasure looking at
each piece of wood. Sizing up which will suit his
mood in that moment. Which will easily yield
to the swing on his axe, and which
will cause him sorrow.

He feels young, carefree, confident and handsome.

He thinks of his wife and the fish moving through
her and the trees gently swaying beneath her skin.

He thinks the world is moving through her now,
just as she has moved through the world.
From being born as a little babe she has grown . . .
into becoming, a fine old woman.

On each swing of his axe he remembers. How they
have lived, so entwined. They have flown through
so many years together.

Two majestic birds.

Upstairs, the elves are back to sitting on the fold.
His wife has turned to snowing.

And he thinks how his wife will soon be carried
by the villagers, buried under the oak
beyond the stream.

. . . the elves sit, just on the fold. As she breathes, they rise up and down with the movement, as if on a gentle sea.

The villagers will sing and tell stories of her. They will tell of her kindness. They will speak of all that she has loved in this world.

The shoemaker will not speak. His weeping will be too great. But he will be thankful to them all.

He holds her cold hand. Kisses her cheek. Whispers that he loves her.

The little people slip into the crook of his neck and together they all nestle in the old wicker chair.

Watching. Waiting. Keeping vigil.

And in the deep, white forest where the snow gently falls, there is a great stillness, a great silence.

And so it is, here, in this humble little cottage, of the shoemaker and his wife.

 Wolf Soup

Blinking, wide eyed. Covered in broken bone.

They are born again. First the woman, then
the young girl. Their faces full of wonder.

The woodcutter stands still, his bloodied axe hanging
at his side. The woman is clutching her shawl. The
girl's hair, vivid red, is matching her shoes.

They stare at one another.
The woodcutter, the woman and the girl.

At their feet lies the enormous wolf.
His fur matted. His paws already stiffening
in the late morning sun.

And they are filled with awe. He is magnificent,
this wild, untamed, clever beast.

'We will make a meal of it,' the woman is whispering.
'Boil the bones, make a soup and, just so there's
no confusion as to who has won and who has lost,
we will eat it up.'

The woodcutter stares at her and she looks to him. And in that moment he is trusting her. Trusting her, and her story and all that she has been through.

So together they are building a fire. Even the young girl helps, fetching sweet pine cones from the forest beyond. Whilst the pot boils, the woman adds onions and herbs from her garden.

In goes the wolf, piece by piece.
The soup bubbling.

They wander down to the river. There they are washing. The woodcutter bathes behind a large boulder so that his private parts remain private.

There is no going back this night. The moon is rising, clouds lying heavy. Everything is hiding, deep in shadow.

They eat the soup. It is strange, at first, to eat the thing that has eaten them, but they make a merry time of it.

And they each recount what has happened as the wolf had, in different ways, taken to them.

The young girl telling of how she had met the wolf in the glade. He had charmed and danced for her, wearing his bright, chequered waistcoat. The words of where she was going had tumbled out of her. When she bent down to pick flowers, the wolf vanished, into the deep woods beyond.

The woman telling of how she'd been working in her garden when a flash of silver collided with her so quickly she had dropped her pitchfork and fallen to the ground. Then she was remembering only darkness and warmth. She had decided to sleep, hoping that when she woke up she'd be back where she began, tending her beans.

When the woodcutter comes to speak, he finds, as always, he can only say but few words. His words are croaky and cracked and he soon stops talking.

The girl and the woman, watching him flounder, quickly withdraw their gaze.

Under the starry sky they sit, fat with wolf soup, each pondering what happened to them that day.

He had charmed and danced for her, wearing his bright chequered waistcoat.

Resting in the quiet solitude of easy company and shared experience. And so the night passes.

When the woodcutter wakes, the first thing he sees, through the window, is the pelt of the wolf hanging on the clothesline. The wolf's mouth is smiling, and with the way the sun catches its eyes, the woodcutter is sure there is a glint in them.

He can hear the laughter of the woman and the girl. He watches them now, coming from the forest, each carrying bunches of wild lavender. He wonders if they are mother and daughter, or grandmother, granddaughter. Since this question involves his speaking, he does not ask.

The woodcutter is dressing and coming out of the house. The woman and the girl lay the lavender at his feet. They are thanking him for saving them.

The woodcutter is overcome with shyness and is moving to be on his way. But the woman stops him. He can see now, she is older. Insisting he eat a good breakfast from out of her pocket, she's unwrapping the wolf's heart.

'I'll be frying it up, along with a good gravy,' she's saying. The girl is licking her lips. Suddenly the woodcutter is overcome with such hunger, his stomach growling and growling. The woman and the girl are laughing.

So they all eat a hearty breakfast and again speak of what happened the day before. Again the woodcutter finds his words croaking and cracking and the others look away, not to add to the embarrassment.

Picking up his axe, the woodcutter makes to be off again, but the woman is calling him back. Carefully she is unpegging the wolf's pelt and laying it upon the woodcutter's back. The wolf's head perches perfectly above his own, like a well worn hat.

'There,' she says. 'A coat to keep you warm, wood-cutter, and to remind you of what you have done.'

She looks to him and he's seeing her fine lines and her beauty. Then she's looking up, into the eyes of the wolf. In that moment, it is as if she has gone back inside the beast, to that warm, dark place, where she had slept.

The girl is lifting her arms and the woodcutter bending and picking her up. He is holding her . . . together with his arms and the wolf's paws, so intermingling they are.

The woodcutter leaves the woman and the girl at the cottage door. They are watching him as he is disappearing into the thick wood beyond.
The man, with the wolf upon his back.

The woodcutter follows the path that will lead him home, back to his old life. He is walking and walking, but there is nothing familiar to him. An exhaustion is creeping over him but he's not stopping. Just falling asleep, yet he keeps on walking.

Pad, pad, pad go his feet.

Then, far away, a stranger thing is happening.
A tree begins to sing, ever so quietly. And the
woodcutter, in his sleep, is following the sound.

Pad, pad, pad go his feet.
Following the sound of the singing tree.

Pad, pad, pad. Sleepwalking through the forest.

Waking, the woodcutter is standing in front of
a tree. A silent, still tree, with dappled colour
along its trunk. The woodcutter, turning round,
now looking at all the trees. They all stand silent
and still. The woodcutter is scratching his head
because he is remembering the singing from his
sleep and nothing is making sense to him.

And the trees are silent still.

The woodcutter is putting his ear and the wolf's
ear against the tree in front of him. He is smiling.
So quiet, so quiet he can hear the tree's song.
A sound from way, way down.

It is a song of wondering.

Twitching, twitching goes the woodcutter's hand.
Something inside him stirring. And the trees from
all around are silent still.

The woodcutter cuts the tree down. Lifting the
tree upon his back, he finds a familiar path. Again
he is making his way home, back to his old life.
With the tree and the wolf upon his back.

Again, he is making his way home, back to his old life. With the tree and the wolf upon his back.

His wife does not recognise him. Even when he has
discarded both the tree and the wolf pelt,
she refuses to believe that he is her husband.
She goes and fetches the second axe that lies
behind the door.

His broken words do nothing to relieve her
torment as she swings the axe wildly at his feet,
screaming, 'Move away, move away!'

He retreats to the furthermost woodshed and lies
there till morning, hoping that a new day will put
things right.

But then his wife is angrier, swinging again with
the axe. He is hiding behind the well where she
cannot find him. When she leaves, the woodcutter
quickly draws a bucket, washes himself, naked,
using the lavender soap.

Scrubbing, scrubbing and when his wife isn't
looking he is fetching fresh clothes, quickly
dressing in the late morning sun.

But she sees him and she is having none of it. She's
throwing all his belongings past the clearing and
screaming banishments so profound that his heart
is breaking. 'You have changed. You have changed!'

Taking the fire stick from the fire, she is laying it
to rest by the cottage door. Quickly the house
catching alight. She is looking at him with a hatred
so terrible the woodcutter is turning his eyes away.
When he turns back, she is gone.

Looking for her, calling, he hears only the birds of the forest answering.

Kneeling down on the forest floor, bending his head, weeping. His home ruined. The woodcutter will have to leave this place. It is a brutal and lasting ending. One he did not see coming.

Taking the tree upon his back, along with the wolf's pelt, carrying the axe. The woodcutter is walking for days in the great forest. Growing hungry, hiding behind trees, waiting for the rabbits to come. Swooping, catching two in a hand, so easily that by the end of the first week he can do it with both eyes closed.

It is the same by the river. Hunched by the river's edge he and the wolf sit and he can see the flash of salmon now coming round the bend. Dabbing his wolf paw into the swirl, pulling out the fish. It fills the woodcutter with a power so strong it is taking his breath away.

Sometimes he is thinking of his wife. Deep in him he knows that she has never forgiven him for the child that never came.

She is, he is thinking, better off without him.

Months pass. The woodcutter finds himself a cave between the river and the forest and so he is living. He is not lonely for he feels that he, the river, and the forest are the same.

Now he's wearing his wolf pelt all the time, only to take it off at night, sleeping on it. In front of his fire.

By day, he flick, flick, flicks at the wood of the tree, his bone knife sharp as he is cutting away at something inside it. And he is singing back to the tree, a sound from way, way down.

At night, he dreams of running in moonlight. His footfall is light, floating above the ground. Faster and faster he is running, his back bent forward, his arms now front legs. Waking, panting, sweating. He is exhilarated by the night's adventures.

A year passes. The woodcutter works away, gently shaping the thing that is inside the tree. It is something he cannot understand and he's knowing not to

By night, he'd dream . . . of running in the moonlight.

question it, but to just let it be. The act of keeping out of the way of it is getting the deed done.

And he's singing from way, way down.
And he's wondering grows stronger and stronger until one day he knows it is finished.

The carving has worked its way through him.
It is a pack of wolves. The beasts, in full flight.
Yet each wolf unique, in and of itself,
moving as one body.

The woodcutter is in awe. What has been made.
There is a fierce power to it. And he's feeling it,
in him.

Packing up his belongings. Carefully wrapping the carving in dried moss. He slings it across his back, under the protection of his wolf pelt.

Walking the forest. Then running it. So fast, so quick, his breath hardly strains. The woodcutter rejoices in the strength of his legs, the lightness of his feet.

Coming upon the cottage, he can hear the woman and the young girl in the forest. He can see them now, picking blackberries. When the young girl sees him, standing in the clearing, she runs to him, shouting, 'Woodcutter, woodcutter.'

His arms wide, she's jumping onto him, and they hold each other so tightly, so happy they are to see each other.

The woman looks to him and blushes and he is pleased by that. That night, she cooks chicken and they feast and laugh, and even though the wood-cutter is a man of few words, the ones he speaks come out as clear as a ringing of a bell, and the woman and the girl are delighting in his company.

After they put the girl to bed, he and the woman sit by the fire. She tells him that her daughter had died, late spring, and that was why her grand-daughter has come to live with her. And through the cracks of the door and the window, the sadness is coming in. And together they are sad, together, they are sad. And the woodcutter feels the sweet-ness of the sadness moving between them.

Blowing out the candle, the woodcutter follows the woman to her bed, his footfall so light in the hall. He takes her and she is gladly taken, with her arching back and the taste of his tongue on her mouth and the fullness of him so deep in her she's rejoicing. How good life is. How good it can be.

In the morning, the woodcutter gives the carving to the young girl and together they are placing it on the shelf above the fire. Then the woodcutter is taking the young girl's hand.

Together they go to the glade.
There in the dappling light,
he's dancing for her.